Stimps

Ro Willoughby

Scripture Union
130 City Road, London EC1V 2NJ

By the same author:

The Castle – for under 6s
Pancake Fingers – for under 6s

To
God's family at
St Andrew's Church, Histon

© Ro Willoughby 1995
First published 1995

ISBN 0 86201 953 2

The right of Ro Willoughby to be identified as author
of this work has been asserted by her in accordance
with the Copyright, Designs and Patents Act 1988.

British Library Cataloguing-in-Publication Data.
A catalogue record for this book is available from the
British Library.

Phototypeset by Intype, London.
Printed and bound in Great Britain by Cox & Wyman
Ltd, Reading.

Contents

STIMPSON and SON

Stimps kicked the Coke can into the gutter and watched it bounce out again into the road, where it lay, waiting for the next passing car to flatten it for ever.

I ought to pick it up, he thought, but then, it wasn't me that dropped it.

He hurried down the High Street in the direction of his dad's shop. He wanted to get home. It had been hard work at school today and these damp, chill autumn days always made him feel miserable. He hoped there wasn't a queue of customers waiting.

His dad's shop was down a wide alley which joined the High Street and the parallel road of shops in town. There were three old shops in the alleyway which was known as Grey's Yard. They huddled close together on one side with the bare brick side wall of the High Street record shop on the other. It was a busy short-cut with many people bustling down it. It sometimes looked like a long litter bin because dust, empty crisp packets and scraps of paper piled up in odd corners or the cracks between the buildings. It was lit by just one lamppost, halfway down, which meant that at night, Grey's Yard was very shadowy. This afternoon, it was still too early for the lamp to be lit.

Before he reached his dad's shop at the far end,

Stimps had to pass the other two shops. First there was Syd's Sandwich Bar, which as usual had all its lights on and was completely empty. Nothing unusual about this. Syd did most of his business at lunch-time.

Stimps sniffed as he went past. He had always felt welcome there from before he could even walk. Among other things Syd sold hot dogs and fried onions and Stimps loved that smell. He sometimes gave Stimps what he called 'a little pick-me-up' – a sausage or a crust of bread or even a cake. But not today, even though the shop was still open. No customers, no smells, no Syd and no 'little pick-me-ups'.

Mrs Jenkins' wool shop, next door, was quite the opposite. It was always grey and unwelcoming. Packets of wool were piled up on three sides of the shop and heaps of old patterns and junk cluttered the floor. The one dimly-lit naked light bulb gave a pale dusty look to the shop. Stimps never went in there. Occasionally he saw Mrs Jenkins locking the door of her shop. She never spoke to him – probably didn't even know who he was – but she would scuttle past him, her shoulders hunched and clutching two big, black bags, one in each hand.

Two years ago there had been talk of her closing down. Stimps had been only seven or eight at the time but he did remember that the firm that owned all three shops had wanted to modernise her shop. The lease had run out or something like that and she was told she'd have to go. Stimps' father had been very angry at this and had written lots of letters of protest. In the end she had stayed. Stimps was vague about the details.

He hurried past her shop, empty as usual, and came to his father's shop. He glanced up at the name over the doorway. STIMPSON and SON it read. But the

'SON' didn't mean Stimps but his dad. The 'STIMP-SON' was his grandfather, who had died ages ago and had left the shop to his son, Stimps' father. A red and white pole stuck out over the entrance.

Stimps' dad was a barber. He only ever cut mens' and boys' hair. They sat in a long line of chairs waiting their turn, just like at the doctor's. There was room for six men to wait. It took twelve and a half minutes on average to have a haircut and the men never complained about having to wait. The men talked to Dad once they were in the chair. But they waited in complete silence, as though they were saving up all they wanted to say until it was their turn.

His dad worked on his own. When it was time for lunch or going home, he just locked up the shop. He had once closed the shop when Stimps had been horribly sick at school. Mum had been out at work in those days and there was no-one else to take him home.

'Do you *mind* taking me home?' Stimps remembered asking his dad as they walked out of the school gate.

'Oh no,' his dad had replied, cheerfully. 'That's one of the great things about having your own business. You close it down when it suits you.'

On that day, Stimps had been very glad of this, because his tummy had felt turned inside out. All he had wanted was to be home in bed.

Today, he wanted to be at home because he was hungry, not because he wanted to be in bed! As he went to push open the door with his bottom, clutching his backpack in his arms, the door suddenly burst open, pulled violently from the inside. Stimps stumbled backwards, knocking into a tall, thin man who brushed past him without a word of apology. Stimps landed with a bump on the floor. The man glanced back at him and was gone.

Stimps recognised him immediately. He had a sandy-coloured moustache which stuck out over his top lip like a bundle of spaghetti sticks. It was the kind of moustache that you didn't forget. The rest of his face was wide and scowling, topped by a bald head.

Stimps' father helped his son stand up and picked up the backpack which had shot under the row of chairs.

'Are you all right, son?' Dad asked.

Stimps nodded, rubbing his elbow. 'That Mr Granville is so rude, isn't he, Dad?' he said. 'What did he want today?' (Mr Granville worked for the firm that owned the three shops in Grey's Yard.)

He sat down on a chair, still rubbing his elbow. His father had obviously finished for the day. No customers were waiting their turn, even though it was still quite early. He locked the door from the inside and came to sit next to his son. Neither of them spoke. It was as though they were both waiting for a haircut and the barber was temporarily absent. Puzzled, Stimps glanced at his dad.

Dad stared down at his feet. He was a solidly-built man with a mass of black, curly hair peppered with grey. He wore gold-framed glasses because he was short-sighted. When he looked at his scissor-work in the large mirror in front of a client, he would screw up his eyes and nose to peer in front of him.

Stimps broke the silence at last. 'Well, what did Mr Granville want?'

Dad stood up wearily.

'Come on. Let's get home', he said, 'and I'll tell you about it in the car.'

Their battered red estate car chuttered its way through the early rush hour. Every driver got in the

way. Traffic lights turned red just as they reached them.
Dad drove, tight-lipped.

'Last month Mr Granville wrote to me about the
business,' he began at last.

(Mr Granville was the agent. He was supposed to
make sure the buildings were repaired if anything went
wrong. He also collected the rent and things like that.
He was usually rude to Mr Stimpson. Stimps thought
him a really horrid man who made life very difficult for
his father.)

'Mr Granville told me the firm want to close down
my shop and modernise it. They want to rent it out to
a "smarter type of business". That's what he said to me
today. I've written to the firm and to my solicitor and
other people who could help. But no-one can do
anything.'

'Is that what they wanted to do to Mrs Jenkins?'
Stimps asked.

'Yes,' Dad said.

'But you managed to get them to change their mind
then. Can't you do that again?'

Dad shook his head. ' 'Fraid not. Legally I haven't
got a leg to stand on. Mr Granville came today to check
that I knew there was nothing to be done. I've got two
more months and then the shop will have to close . . .
just before Christmas.'

The car drew up outside their house. Father and son
walked into the house gloomily. Mum was cooking tea,
banging saucepans and making a lot of clatter. Stimps
went straight up to his room. Dad would want to talk
to Mum on his own.

He slumped down on his bed. How would Dad find
another job? Old-fashioned barbers like his dad were
unusual these days. Dad was always saying that hairdressing salons for men *and* women could be found

11

everywhere. His sort of shop was much less common.

Stimps stared miserably out of the window. He could tell from Mr Granville's face when he knocked him over that he had come with bad news. Why was Mr Granville such a horrid man? Why did he treat Dad so awfully?

The more Stimps thought about it, the more churned up he became. It all seemed so unfair. Why was it only Dad's shop and not Mrs Jenkins' or Syd's Sandwich Bar? Anger began to bubble inside.

It must be time for tea. He jumped down the stairs two at a time. But in the doorway of the kitchen he froze. All signs of tea had disappeared. His mother was sitting on the kitchen stool, clutching a scrunched-up handkerchief in her hands. Both her eyes looked red and blotchy. His father was leaning against the cupboard, arms folded, looking very grim.

Mum wiped her eyes again and sniffed. Stimps didn't know what to do. He couldn't bear to see Mum upset. His head began to thump. All the muscles in his neck tensed up. His head felt like a balloon, blown up so much it was about to burst. He had got to *do* something.

Suddenly, not knowing why, he dashed to the back door, yanked it open and made for the bike shed. He needed air. He needed space. He jumped on his bike and set off furiously down the road.

'Come back, son!' he heard his dad call from the back door step. 'Where are you going?'

Stimps didn't answer. He wasn't going to stop for anyone!

The Grandma

It was dark and drizzling as Stimps pedalled furiously down the road. He hadn't had time to put on his coat. He wiped the rain from his forehead. He didn't know where he was going. He didn't care!

'Mr Granville can't *do* this to Dad,' he shouted in his head. 'The shop has belonged to Grandpa and Dad for years and years. Everyone in town knows STIMPSON and SON, the barber down the alleyway. Mr Granville has never forgiven Dad after that business with Mrs Jenkins' wool shop. He's getting his revenge. How can he demand that Dad close down the shop in two months' time?'

He was pedalling very fast, not thinking where he was going; so fast that he whizzed right through a deep puddle at the side of the road. Water sprayed out on either side of the wheel and soaked his trousers.

He pictured his mum in tears. She found life hard enough as it was. They never had much money. It would be even worse now. Nothing was fair! (If he hadn't been pedalling he would have lashed out with his foot at the nearest lamppost in sheer anger.)

Stimps thought of Syd and the Sandwich Bar. Syd always had a good story to tell and food leftovers on offer. Stimps had always told Syd about the important things in his life, like getting the new mountain bike, or his big sister leaving home to be a nurse. Stimps had moved into her big bedroom. Syd had laughed.

'Keep it tidy, young man,' he'd said. 'Lots more space can mean lots more clutter.' (Syd's shop was always very tidy and clean.)

I shall have to visit Syd in the holidays, Stimps thought sadly.

That made Stimps want to kick something again in anger. Why had Mr Granville only picked on Dad's shop? Why not Mrs Jenkins' and Syd's Sandwich Bar? It just wasn't fair!

Surely Dad could do something else. Couldn't he write to the MP? Couldn't he . . .? But he'd said he had done all he could.

'Hey!' yelled a voice in the darkness. 'Watch where you're going!'

Stimps swerved, just missing another lamppost. Now where was he? He slowed down and stopped to get his breath back.

The rain had soaked right through to his skin. He felt cold, tired and squelchy. It looked as though he was near the football ground. Wasn't Pete's new house near here? He'd been round there with several friends from school only last Saturday. Perhaps Pete would be in.

Pete was in Stimps' class at school. He had recently moved to this part of town because his grandma had come to live with them and they needed a bigger house. He hadn't changed schools because he and Stimps were in Year 6 which meant that next year they were going to change schools anyway.

Stimps remembered where Pete lived, although he had never been there in the dark. The house looked different but the light was on. Someone must be in. He rang the bell.

After what seemed ages the door opened a chink.

'Hello,' said an old-sounding voice. 'Who is it?'

Stimps took a step backwards and nearly fell off the step. This must be The Grandma.

'I'm . . . I'm a friend of Pete's,' he stammered. 'I . . . er . . . I go to school with him. My name's Robert.' (He always used his proper name when talking to an adult.)

'What do you want?' the voice said.

Stimps could just make out the top half of The Grandma's head and a hand clutching the door. (Stimps was already calling her 'The Grandma' in his head. After all, what do you call someone else's grandparent?)

'I got lost round here on my bike and I'm very wet and is Pete in?' This all came out rather quickly.

The half-head and hand disappeared. There was a clanking sound as a chain was undone and the door opened wide.

Stimps had been right. It was The Grandma; at least, it was an old lady, with a round face surrounded by short white hair.

'Is Pete in?' Stimps asked again rather nervously.

'Yes,' she replied. 'Come in. You look wet through.'

Stimps squelched into the hall where he stood, uncomfortably.

'Take your jumper off', said The Grandma, 'and come into the kitchen. And take your shoes off!' Then she called up the stairs, 'Pete, you've got a visitor!'

The Grandma sounded just like Mrs Whiteman, his teacher at school. She hobbled stiffly into the kitchen. Stimps pulled off his jumper with difficulty. It stuck to him like an orange skin. He ripped off his shoes, not bothering to undo the laces, and then his socks. He left them in a wet pile by the front door and followed The Grandma. A door banged and someone bounded down the stairs. Pete burst into the room.

'What are *you* doing here, Stimps?' he asked, gazing at his wet friend. 'You look like a dog who's just fallen into the river.'

'Do you want a cup of tea?' The Grandma asked.

'Yes please,' Stimps said. He was particularly fond of a mug of tea. Very few of his friends liked tea as much as he did, which always surprised him. Even Pete didn't!

'And are you hungry?' The Grandma asked.

Stimps nodded. A drip of rain plopped from his fringe on to the table.

She picked up a large loaf of white bread which she began to cut into enormous wedges. She spread them with margarine and put them on a plate which she placed in front of Stimps. Cheese and jam joined the plate on the table, followed by a large mug of tea. For a lady who moved so stiffly, she did all this very quickly.

'Now eat that up,' she ordered, 'and then you can tell us why a boy like you is riding round in the pouring rain at this time of night.'

Stimps took several gulps of tea and realised his anger had dried up, at least for the moment. It was the only thing about him which had dried up. His wet trousers felt horrible and he noticed a wet patch on the floor underneath his trouser legs. But as he ate, he began to feel warmer.

All the time he was chewing he tried to work out how he could explain things. His mind was a blank. At last, The Grandma came to the rescue. 'You've run away from home, haven't you?' she said.

Stimps looked at her horrified. Was that what she had been thinking? Was that what Pete thought? That he had run away? Was that what Mum and Dad would think?

16

'Oh, no,' he said, quickly. 'It's nothing like that. Pete will tell you, my dad's got a barber's shop.'

Then he told them about Mr Granville's latest visit to Dad and how the shop had got to be closed in two months' time, just before Christmas.

'He's a really horrid man. Looks like he's scowling all the time. It's something to do with his moustache which sticks out. And he barks at you like a dog. He's very tall and thin. He's like a giant.'

'So what made you come here?' Pete asked, when his friend had finished.

'I don't know really, but I was so angry', Stimps said, 'I thought my head would explode or I might smash something. I felt I needed to *do* something,' and he banged his fists on the table as he remembered. 'It just isn't fair!'

'Something like that happened to Gran,' Pete said. 'Didn't it, Gran?'

The Grandma nodded.

'She'd lived in her house for years,' Pete explained. 'And one day a letter came saying the council wanted to build a new ring road right through her block of houses. They'd give her money for the house but she'd have to live somewhere else. That's why she came to live with us.'

'Did you want to move?' Stimps asked The Grandma.

She shook her head, opening her already-wide bright blue eyes even wider. 'Oh, no. I'd lived in that house ever since I had got married. I knew all the neighbours, had lots of friends and had managed to keep the garden nice after Pete's grandfather died. It was my home.'

'So what happened?' Stimps asked.

'Well, we wrote lots of letters and complained and complained. No-one in the road wanted to move. And the environmental people helped us too . . . signed a petition, you know, that sort of thing. We even went on the local television news. But nothing changed. And then my legs got really bad. It's hard for me to get about now. So Pete's mum said I'd better come and live with them.'

Stimps felt miserable. If all those people hadn't managed to change anything, what hope was there for Dad?

'When you first heard, did you feel like *your* head was going to burst, like I did just now? Did you want to hit something hard?' (Stimps couldn't really imagine The Grandma smashing up anything.)

'Oh, yes,' she said calmly. 'I marched up and down my front room shouting at the wall. It seemed so unfair. One day I got so cross I knocked over a little table with a vase on. It smashed and the splinters of glass, flowers and water scattered all over the carpet. It was an awful mess. And just as I was wondering how I was going to clean it up, the doorbell rang and a friend arrived. She helped me tidy up. And I talked to her and cried and talked some more. And then we both told God how angry we felt and asked him to do something.'

'And did he?' Stimps asked, surprised. He couldn't see why anyone would want to ask God anything.

'In a way, yes,' The Grandma said. 'I stopped feeling so angry. And now my legs have got so bad I'm sure it's the best thing that I'm here, even though I do still miss my home and friends and neighbours. Not that the house is there any more. The bulldozers knocked it down a month ago.'

A sad smile came over her face.

'But we do like having you here, Gran,' Pete said, putting an arm round his grandma.

'I think you'd better get home, now you've finished

your tea,' The Grandma said, struggling to her feet. 'Ring your parents and tell them you're here?'

Dad, of course, said he'd fetch Stimps and put the bike in the back of the old red estate car.

'Just stay where you are. Don't disappear again,' he said down the phone. He sounded relieved.

I'm sure he'll be furious once I'm home, Stimps thought.

He sat in the kitchen listening to The Grandma and Pete. But he wasn't really listening. His thoughts were elsewhere.

The doorbell rang and it was at that precise moment Stimps came to a decision. Dad had done all he could but that didn't stop STIMPSON the GRANDSON from taking action!

'Just you watch out, Mr Granville!' he muttered.

Trouble at school

It was still dark when Stimps woke the next morning. He turned over, burying his head under his duvet. He didn't want the day to begin. There was a heavy lump in his chest and he couldn't think why.

For several minutes he lay, his brain scrambled in the way it often is when you first wake up. What was the matter with today? This wasn't like him at all. What had happened yesterday?

Yesterday! He flipped over sharply on to his back. Of course! Yesterday! Dad had got to leave the shop! He groaned as the memory of yesterday flooded into his mind. Dad had done all he could so it was up to him, Robert Stimpson, to take action.

Anger began to bubble again inside, along with a feeling of hopelessness. How could *he* change anything? No-one ever listened to a ten-year-old boy, especially one who couldn't always put into words exactly what he wanted to say.

He reached out for a piece of paper by his bed. He'd begun to make up a letter to send to the *Evening News*, the local paper. That was one thing Dad hadn't done. The paper often investigated readers' problems. He'd heard Mum talk about it. They might be interested.

He reread the start of the letter and sighed. No-one

would be interested in the closure of STIMPSON and SON. Lots of small shops in town were up For Sale or To Let. Dad's shop was no different.

Stimps lay clutching the letter under his duvet. He gazed up at the ceiling, staring at nothing and tried to think. But he could only think how unfair all this was. His thoughts went round and round and round.

He must have dozed off because his mother found him two hours later, still lying on his back, still holding a crumpled piece of paper.

'Time to get up, Robert,' she said, pulling the duvet off his face. 'What've you got there?'

'Nothing Mum,' he mumbled.

She pulled back the curtains.

'Mum, is there really nothing else Dad can do?' Stimps asked.

She turned towards him and in the grey light from the window, Stimps could see just how pale her face was. She obviously hadn't slept well last night.

'No,' she replied, shaking her head. 'He feels like an ant about to be squashed by a giant's foot. Nothing can be done. Mr Granville has made that quite clear.'

Over breakfast the radio was on. No-one needed to talk. As Stimps cleared away his cereal bowl he asked his father, 'Who is it that actually owns the shop, Dad?'

'MT Trott,' was the reply. 'It's a big firm that owns lots of property in town. They buy up run-down shops and offices and then modernise them. It's on old family firm that has made a lot of money over the years. Mr Granville is one of their agents. I've never met MT Trott myself.'

Stimps sucked his top lip thoughtfully. He had had two ideas about saving the shop. Either he could block off both ends of the alleyway with an electric fence to stop the men who were employed to alter Dad's shop from getting there. But there were lots of objections to that. For one thing, Syd wouldn't like that! Or he might print some handouts asking for support. He could give them to shoppers on Saturday, like other people did. But that would be expensive and he knew most shoppers threw their handout into the nearest bin, if they didn't drop it straight on to the ground. By the time he'd got to school he was no nearer a sensible plan of action.

Pete was taking off his coat as Stimps walked into the cloakroom. He didn't say anything about last night, just grinned at Stimps in a secretive sort of way. Stimps didn't want to talk about last night. In fact he didn't want to talk to anybody.

He was in no mood for work at all. He just couldn't concentrate. He finished a page of his maths workbook which Mrs Whiteman happened to mark straightaway. He'd got the whole page wrong and had to repeat it.

Before lunch there was a time for silent reading. Stimps stared at a page of print for ten minutes but didn't read a word. He kept thinking about Mr Granville and trying to do something. He felt angry and upset inside.

After lunch Mrs Whiteman told Stimps' group to paint a scene of peace and quiet, using powder paints. It could be anywhere they liked.

Stimps, feeling anything but peaceful, decided to paint his bedroom which had become his when his sister had gone to be a nurse. It was his den where he could escape from the rest of the family. He wasn't often disturbed there so, for him, it was a most peaceful place. He mixed up the colours and began to paint.

But it wouldn't go right. His painting made the room dull and lifeless. The corner was the wrong shape, not like it really was. He painted over part of a wall and began again. But this made it even worse. And the colour was all wrong. It wasn't peaceful at all. And all the time, he was picturing his mother's face that morning – sad, pale and tired. She had no hope that things could get better.

Stimps began to jab his paintbrush on his painting, making dark splodges appear all over his bedroom, as though angry rain was falling into his room through the ceiling. Suddenly his own anger bubbled up and out. He swung his right arm over the painting, knocking over the paint pots which spilled their coloured liquids over the other childrens' paintings.

'Stimps!' they all shouted.

'You twit!'

'What did you do that for?'

Stimps dashed into the cloakroom where he sat on the floor in the corner, partly hidden by coats, except for his feet. He was going to be in big trouble now.

He was right. Mrs Whiteman stormed after him, going straight for the corner of the cloakroom.

'What is the meaning of this, Robert?' she demanded.

Stimps peeped through the layers of coats which hid him. She was standing with her arms folded, staring at him.

'Come out from there!' she ordered.

Stimps scrambled to his feet. How could he explain?

She softened a little. 'It's not like you to do something stupid like that,' she said. And that was true. Stimps wasn't one of the really naughty children in the class.

'I know,' he muttered again.

'Well, are you going to explain?'

Stimps paused. What could he tell her?

'It's my dad,' he said at last. 'He's going to be out

of work and . . .'

Mrs Whiteman dropped her folded arms.

'I'm sorry about that,' she said.

'And I was thinking about him just now and then I got angry.'

Mrs Whiteman had had a busy day and just didn't have any time to listen to Stimps. She needed to get back into the classroom.

'We'll talk about it after school if you like,' she said. 'But come into the classroom now and clear up this mess.'

But Stimps did *not* want to go back into the classroom. The other children would be furious with him. He had *ruined* their afternoon's work. So he stayed where he was, leaning against the coats, staring out of the window.

Five minutes later, Mrs Whiteman returned. She was a tall, thin lady about the same age as his mother. Most of the children thought she was OK as teachers go, but she did shout at them when she didn't know what to do. This was one of those occasions.

'Robert Stimpson,' she shouted, 'I asked you to clean up the mess you made. But you've just stood here, feeling sorry for yourself. It's not good enough and it's not fair on the other children.'

Mention of 'fairness' was unfortunate. Stimps was usually very polite but the word 'fairness' acted like a spark to set a fire alight. He muttered loudly, 'Don't talk to me about what's fair!' and pushed past her to march down the corridor.

'Robert Stimpson, come here!' she shouted after him but he didn't stop. He didn't know where he was going but he wasn't going back into the classroom.

The timing of his march could not have been worse, for round the corner came Mr Brooke, the headteacher. Stimps was trapped. Mrs Whiteman behind him, Mr Brooke in front.

'What's all this?' Mr Brooke asked sharply.

Stimps froze as though in the middle of a game of musical statues. Mrs Whiteman spoke from behind him. She didn't explain about Dad's job, just complained about Stimps' rudeness. Mr Brooke went on and on to Stimps about respecting teachers and working hard and all that sort of thing. Stimps had heard it all before, dozens of times. In the end Mr Brooke said, 'You can spend the next two playtimes standing outside my door.'

It wasn't as bad as it might have been because it rained heavily during the next two playtimes so Stimps didn't miss out on any football in the playground. It was during the second playtime that he finally settled on his next move. He was amazed he hadn't thought of it before.

He would go to see Syd of the Sandwich Bar. He was bound to have some ideas about what could be done to save Dad's shop.

Mr Granville lays his plans

Mr Charles Granville stretched out his long legs and yawned. It had been a difficult day at work. His new boss at MT Trott's didn't make things easy. He pushed his empty plate away from him and sighed.

But the barber's shop in Grey's Yard was troubling him. Mr Stimpson wasn't going to make any trouble. He was sure of that. Closing the shop down to modernise it was fairly straightforward. Everything was running smoothly. Plans had already been drawn up for the new shop. Several people were interested in letting it. A small but smart ladies' clothes shop seemed the most likely. That would make an improvement to Grey's Yard. And Mr Stimpson wouldn't be able to cause any more trouble. He had never liked that barber.

But Mr Granville still felt unsettled. He thoughtfully stroked his moustache. (This was the moustache which Stimps thought stuck out like sticks of spaghetti!) Why should he be troubled about it? He had a dread that something would go wrong. He couldn't explain it.

'I know it's hard for the barber, but you can't let peoples' feelings stand in the way of progress,' Mr Granville said out loud to the empty room. (He lived on his own in a small flat which belonged to MT Trott.) 'No small barber's shop can stand in the way of a giant property-owning firm like MT Trott.'

Mr Granville got out his files and settled down for an evening's work. He was not in the habit of feeling sorry for other people.

The ant meets the giant

The lights were on in Syd's Sandwich Bar when Stimps walked down the alley that evening on his way home from school. A couple of lads were drinking Coke at the table by the window. They were laughing over a newspaper report.

Stimps hesitated before going inside. Surely Dad would have talked with Syd about what had happened. But Dad hadn't said so. Stimps took a deep breath. He couldn't put it off till tomorrow. He pushed open the door. He could hear singing in the kitchen behind the shop. Stimps walked straight into the kitchen. He was no ordinary customer. *He* didn't have to wait at the counter to be served.

'Hello young Stimps!' Syd called out cheerfully, unpacking some food from a big box. 'Haven't seen you for ages. What you been up to?'

Stimps sniffed. He always did this whenever he came into Syd's kitchen.

'Have a doughnut,' Syd said pointing to a packet on the side. 'And help yourself to a Coke from outside.'

Stimps didn't bother with a plate. He held the doughnut up well above his mouth, to catch the stream of red jam which oozed out as he squeezed it. He gave himself a moustache of sugar and then licked his lips thoroughly.

He filled a glass with Coke. He always felt better once food was inside his stomach. Back in the kitchen, he perched on top of the kitchen stool.

'Well, where have you been?' Syd asked.

Syd spent all his lunch-time talking to customers over the bar and was always asking questions but didn't often wait for the answer! He just loved talking. He started work early in the morning, long before STIMP-SON and SON's was open because he had to buy his food from the wholesaler and then come to the shop to make and wrap up sandwiches. These were sandwiches for the 'can't-stop workers' as he called them – the people who rushed into the sandwich bar to buy their lunch, didn't bother what kind they chose and dashed out again, clutching a neat packet of two tri-angular sandwiches. These people had no time to talk. Syd occasionally grumbled about them. But not too much, since they made up most of his customers. He preferred the people who stayed to chat.

But on this occasion he wanted an answer from Stimps. 'So where have you been?' Syd asked again.

'Nowhere much,' Stimps replied.

'Haven't seen your dad for some time either,' Syd went on.

Stimps took a deep breath. 'Haven't you heard, then?' he blurted out.

'Heard what?' Syd asked, puzzled.

'Hasn't Dad told you?'

'Told me what?'

Syd stopped unpacking his box of food and stared at Stimps.

'About Dad having to leave the shop because the shop is going to be modernised. Dad's got to be gone in less than two months, just before Christmas. Mr Granville says there's nothing Dad can do to stop it.'

'What!'

Without any explanation, Syd yelled, 'You stay here!' and dashed out of the kitchen, into the shop and out into the alley. Stimps guessed he was going into STIMPSON and SON.

Stimps stood behind the counter, hoping someone would come in to order a drink. He loved serving customers. The two lads in the window left, scraping their chairs and still laughing, and banged the door behind them. No new customers came in.

After what seemed hours, Syd returned.

'Your dad wants to see you,' was all he said, as he headed back into the kitchen. Stimps followed him. He had come to ask Syd for advice. He wasn't going to leave without it.

'Can't *you* do something?' Stimps asked. 'Surely *you* can think of something we can do.'

Syd shook his head, scowling. He was unpacking another box, thumping bags of sugar onto the side with such a bang that Stimps was afraid the sugar would burst out.

'There's nothing to be done,' Syd said sharply. 'We've been this way before. They didn't manage to get Mrs Jenkins out but that was two years ago. Things have changed.'

'But can't you and Dad and Mrs Jenkins work together on this?' Stimps asked. Despair crept into his voice. 'Mum said it was like an ant meeting a giant. Syd, you've got to come up with an idea. You've got to help us.'

His voice was getting higher as he spoke. He felt like bursting into tears. Surely Syd could think of something they could do. But Syd just shook his head.

Stimps pictured The Grandma. She'd stamped up and down her room and smashed her favourite vase *and* written letters. *She'd* done everything she could. And had even asked God to help. Funny sort of thing to do but she thought that had made a difference.

Disappointed, Stimps made for the door. Syd was obviously too upset to talk. Perhaps they could talk about it tomorrow.

It was only ten long strides between the Sandwich Bar and Dad's shop. Stimps had measured the distance many times. But today, on the third step he stopped. If The Grandma could pray, he was going to try too. But how do you start a prayer?

'Our Father, which art in Heaven . . .' he muttered.

That sounded too much like school assembly. He didn't understand it. Anyway, that reminded him of Mr Brooke and he'd had quite enough of Mr Brooke for one day.

He took three more strides, stopped again and muttered, very quickly, 'Oh God, help me.'

Four more strides and he was on the step of STIMP-SON and SON. I hope you heard that, God, he thought and pushed open the door.

Dad was sweeping the floor. Business was over for the day.

'I told Syd the full story,' Dad said brushing steadily. 'I hadn't wanted to get him involved before because he'd immediately think his sandwich bar would be the next shop to close.'

'And could that be true?' Stimps asked.

Dad shrugged.

'Possibly, Robert,' he sighed as he propped up his broom in the cupboard. 'Now come on. There's an empty hairdressing salon just outside town. We'll have a look at it on the way home. Who knows? It could be just right for us.' He was trying to sound positive but Stimps wasn't fooled.

They drove out to the edge of town to a small village, on the coast road. It was getting dark. Hardly the best time to be looking at an empty shop. The man from the estate agent's was waiting for them, with the key to unlock the shop.

'The electricity is switched off,' he said, 'but I've brought my torch and it's not quite dark. It will give you some idea of what it's like.'

'How long has it been empty?' Dad asked.

'Oh, some time,' the estate agent answered vaguely.

It looked as though it had been empty for years and years. It was a shop which had been made out of the downstairs of an ordinary house. The front garden was paved over but the paving stones were cracked with large clumps of weeds sprouting along the cracks. The front window was also cracked, from top to bottom.

Inside there was a horrid musty smell. Dust coated everything. The furniture was out-of-date, a chair with only two legs lay upside down, the basins and mirrors were cracked. The man's torchlight made the salon look like a disused rubbish tip.

Dad caught Stimps' eye and grimaced. This would never do. Back in the car, they both had lots to say about how awful it was.

'You can't work there, Dad,' Stimps said.

'You're right,' his father replied. 'It would need so many improvements. And there weren't many people living round there. I can't imagine where customers would come from. I'd have to learn to cut ladies' hair as well and I'm not sure I want to do that.'

'Haven't they any other shops for sale?' Stimps asked.

'No, unless we rent one of the many empty shops in town and convert it into a barber's shop. But I don't want to do that. I just don't know what we'll do.' Dad shook his head in despair.

Back home they told Mum about it. She shook her head just like Dad. Stimps went up to his room, his den, and flopped down on his bed. It was all so hopeless.

He must have dozed off to sleep, because he was surprised to find himself crawling along a muddy path. He kept falling over. He seemed to have lost his arms because he had thin legs at the front and back and couldn't balance on his legs in the middle. Where was he? And more to the point, what was he? He lifted one leg in the air and wobbled dangerously. He put it down quickly. Had he really become what he began to suspect? Yes, he'd become an ant. He'd have to get used to having six legs.

Ahead of him he saw funny-looking trees, just tall sticks of green with a point on the end. No leaves, nowhere for birds to land. Never seen trees like this before. They looked like grass.

Suddenly the ground around him trembled. He scurried towards the 'trees' which were at the side of the path. The ground trembled again. Thud! Thud! What was it? An earthquake? His heart thumped as loud as the approaching thud. What could he do? Where could he escape?

He looked up and far above him saw a floating hedge. Below it was a stretch of blue material upon which was written the words 'MT Trott'. His eye travelled down to a hairy knee and on further to what seemed like an enormous skin-coloured hillock. Stimps gasped. He realised what he was looking at. This was a giant. The hedge was his beard. The hillock was a foot. And what was more, this giant was about to tread on him.

The knee moved. There was another mighty thud. Stimps just stood where he was, frozen. He couldn't move forward or backward. He was stuck, helpless.

Gingerly he lifted his face upwards. The hairy knee had moved on. It was past him. The hedge floated away. MT Trott was gone. Phew! Stimps had survived. He hadn't been crushed by the giant. His spindly legs wobbled uncontrollably.

He woke, sweat standing on his forehead. His imagination had got the better of him. Fancy dreaming about becoming an ant!

But as he went downstairs for his tea, he realised, with a scary feeling, what his next move should be. He was going to have to meet MT Trott in person. He didn't know how, but he was going to try.

'I'll show you what kind of an ant I am,' he muttered. 'MT Trott, here I come!'

Stimps explores enemy territory

It's one thing to have an idea but quite another to turn that idea into action. Stimps, among other feelings, felt very lonely. Syd had been no help and his parents seemed to have given up the fight. As they saw it, in a few weeks time, STIMPSON and SON would go out of business. And Mr Stimpson was looking for another job, but in a half-hearted way. Jobs were hard to find. Stimps was sure they talked to each other about the business but they never mentioned it to him.

Pete seemed to have forgotten about his night visit. Stimps wished Pete would ask him about his dad, because he needed to talk to someone.

One lunch-time the following week, he got his opportunity. That morning Mrs Whiteman had been in a bad mood. After taking the register she had glared at the class sitting on the carpet at her feet.

'Yesterday evening,' she said sternly, 'I spent half an hour unblocking the sink. When I removed the U-bend and all the bunged-up water had flowed out, I discovered eight small paintbrushes stuck fast down the pipe. I repeat, *eight* paintbrushes. Somebody, and I don't know who, has been deliberately poking paint-brushes through the plug-hole. It's a disgrace. I want two volunteers to tidy up the painting area in the class-room this lunch-time. And after that, there will be no art work for a week, which I know will be disappointing for you all. If the person who was stupid enough to do such a thing owns up, I might change my mind.'

Most people had a good idea who it was but no-one owned up. It was Stimps and Pete who volunteered to clean out the cupboard where the paints were kept. Stimps grabbed his opportunity.

'Look Pete,' he said, washing up pots in mucky brown water, 'you haven't forgotten about what's going to happen to my dad's shop, have you?'

Pete shook his head. 'Of course not,' he said.

'Well,' Stimps went on, 'I've decided *I'm* going to have to meet the owner of the shop and tell him how unfair it is.'

'Why doesn't your dad do that?' Pete asked.

'He's done all he can and can't see what else there is to be done.'

'How are *you* going to get to see the owner?' Pete asked.

'I don't know. I just wondered if you had any ideas.'

Pete put down the pots he was wiping and sat on the edge of the table, thinking.

'Who owns the shop?' he asked.

'MT Trott, a property-owning firm in town. They own masses of property in town . . . all three shops down Grey's Yard.'

Pete frowned. 'Have you got their address?'

'Yes, I found it in the phone book,' Stimps answered.

'And is MT Trott the actual man who's the boss?'

'I think so,' Stimps said. He really didn't know much about MT Trott, himself. Dad had never told him much.

'Why don't we go and have a look at MT Trott's offices in town and see what we can find out?' Pete said.

Stimps' face brightened up. That was an excellent idea.

The next Saturday the two boys met in town outside the library. Stimps hadn't wanted to tell his mum exactly why he was so keen to go into town so he just told her his books were nearly overdue at the central library. He somehow felt she wouldn't approve if she knew what he was up to. Pete told his mum the same story. It was sort of true.

MT Trott's offices were in Numbers 5–9, Glate Street, which was behind the library. Stimps had brought a street map of the town. The boys found it with no difficulty.

The main entrance had three wide, marble steps leading to a wide wooden door. To the side of the door was a highly-polished, brass plaque announcing, 'MT Trott Properties'.

The boys crossed over the road to have a look at the upstairs floors. Nothing out of the ordinary to be seen.

'Let's have a look at the back,' Stimps suggested.

'You sound like a burglar planning a break-in,' Pete said.

The back of the building was easily reached. A driveway went down the side of Number 9, which led to a line of garages and some car-parking spaces. The building had once been three three-storey houses which were joined together but were now just one set of offices. The back gardens had been turned into a big car-park. An iron fire escape ran from the top floor of each house to the ground. The building had one back entrance.

'Would help if you wanted to get away quickly,' Stimps muttered.

'Stimps, you're sounding more and more like a burglar,' Pete said. 'What are you thinking of doing?'

'I just don't know,' Stimps replied. 'But I'm thinking.'

The car-park was empty because it was a Saturday. Stimps wanted to know if the back door was open all the time on a weekday. Did MT Trott really exist? If so, which was his office? Did he come to work by car? What did he look like? Who else worked there? He had so many questions.

'How can I find out about MT Trott?' he wondered, gazing up at the building.

Pete had been wandering over the car-park, looking at the markings. In one parking space, in faded-white letters he read,

M T TROTT

'Come here!' he yelled to Stimps.

Stimps raced over to where his friend was standing. He stared down at the ground, frowning.

'So MT Trott drives a car,' he said.

But that didn't get them very far. The two boys stood side by side on the empty car-park as though they were trying to decide what game to play. But this was no game. This was serious.

'I know what you've got to do,' Pete said suddenly. 'You've got to come here on a weekday when the offices are open and see what it's like. And then talk to that horrible Mr Granville yourself. He can't stop you phoning him up. And talking to *him* might give you some ideas about what you can do next.'

'Well, I suppose that's possible,' Stimps said, doubtfully. 'I could get Mr Granville's number from Dad. Mind you, I don't think he'll want to talk to *me*.'

'Could I see your dad's shop?' Pete asked. 'I've never been there.'

'Of course,' Stimps said. 'I'll take you to Syd's Sandwich Bar next door as well.'

Syd was busy but pleased to see the boys. He slipped two chocolate bars over the counter but had no time to talk.

'Whose shop is this?' Pete asked, as they went past Mrs Jenkins' wool shop.

The shop was as gloomy as ever. Stimps was about to explain about Mrs Jenkins when the door opened and out she came, a bent, little lady in her usual overlarge grey coat, with a woolly black hat pulled down over her ears. She fumbled with the key, locking up the shop for the day. She stared straight through the two boys as she scuttled past them, clasping her two black carrier bags. Stimps thought how thin she looked, much thinner than when he'd last seen her.

I wonder if she knows what's going to happen to Dad's shop, he thought.

'Funny lady,' Stimps said. 'I don't know how she manages to keep her shop open. I've never seen anyone in there buying anything.'

At home that evening, while his dad was watching television, he peeped inside the box where the shop business papers were kept. Dad had never allowed him or his sister to look inside this box. It was top secret. Stimps felt bad about doing it now but, he reasoned, he was only looking for the phone number of Mr Granville. He'd got to find it.

He flicked through the papers as quickly as he could. There were notes about this and that. Nothing very interesting. Ah, here was an important-looking letter! It came from Mr Granville with headed MT TROTT notepaper and a telephone number, 234869. Mr Granville must use the same number as the office.

Stimps read:

12 October 1994

Dear Mr Stimpson,

With reference to your letter, 27 September 1994, I am sorry to inform you there is no possibility of a reconsideration of our decision to modernise the shop and flat above 12 Grey's Yard. You are required to vacate the shop premises by 15 December 1994. May I remind you, as the contract states, three months' notice can be given on either side of intention to end the contract and your notice was served on 16 September 1994.

Yours sincerely,

C. Granville

Charles Granville
(Agent for MT Trott)

Stimps frowned. He didn't understand all the letter, but it was written in a thoroughly nasty tone. What a horrid man Mr Granville was. Stimps remembered how he had knocked him over in the shop doorway. Still, at least he'd now got Mr Granville's telephone number. He scribbled the number down on a scrap of paper.

Carefully, he slid the letter back where he'd found it, closed the lid of the box and tiptoed out of the room. He didn't know why he was tiptoeing. The television was quite loud enough to drown any noise he might make. But Stimps felt guilty. He shouldn't have looked in his dad's box.

He went to bed early. It was easier to make plans in his den.

'Is Robert all right?' he heard his mother say as he

went upstairs. 'He seems to be very secretive these days.'

'He's upset about the shop,' he heard his father's deep voice.

I'm more than upset, Stimps thought. I'm angry. This whole business is so unfair!

I suppose I shall have to miss school on Monday, he thought, if I'm to see what happens at MT Trott's in the daytime. He couldn't think of any other way round it. I wish Pete would come with me but we can't both miss school or Mrs Whiteman will suspect something.

He pulled up his pyjama trousers and sighed. This was so important he'd have to risk it. But what if Mr Brooke finds out . . . That was a thought almost worse than death!

Caught out

Over Monday breakfast Stimps tried to act as normal. He'd never before dreamt of deliberately missing school. He chewed his piece of toast, although it tasted like cardboard and stuffed his packed lunch into his backpack as usual. He left the house at half past eight.

As he got towards the corner he heard a bus coming up from behind. He didn't want to miss it so he raced for the bus stop, reaching it just in time. He flopped down breathless, on a seat at the back, hoping no-one on the bus would know him.

He fingered the phone card Mum had given him a few months back, in case of an emergency. He'd never used it before and wasn't quite sure how to. Still, there was a first time for everything. All the way into town, he practised what he would say to Mr Granville.

(*'I'm making an enquiry about the barber's shop in Grey's Yard. It's been there a long time. I wonder, can you tell me why it is closing down . . . ?'*)

Once in town, he found a phone box just by the library. He pulled out his card and the crumpled piece of paper with Mr Granville's telephone number on.

By the time he had understood how to work a phone card, there were two other people queuing up to use the same phone. Cautiously he pushed his card in the slot and dialled the number. 234 . . . he glanced at his crumpled paper . . . 869. He hoped Mr Granville was in his office. The phone began to ring. One. Two. Three. Four. Five. Click.

'Good morning. MT Trott Properties. Can I help you?' It was a woman's voice.

Stimps cleared his throat. His heart was thudding.

'I want to speak to Mr Granville,' he said in as deep a voice as he could manage.

'Putting you through,' said the receptionist's voice.

Stimps waited. Click . . . click.

'Charles Granville speaking,' came a man's gruff voice.

'Ah, ah Mr Granville, I . . . er . . .'

'Who's that speaking?' Mr Granville barked impatiently.

'I . . . want to . . . it's about Grey's Yard . . .' Stimps stuttered.

'Yes?'

'I . . . er . . . need . . . .'

Click. The phone went dead. Stimps took the receiver away from his ear and held it in his hand, dazed. Mr Granville had put the phone down on him. He sighed. Whenever he got nervous he couldn't get his words out straight. It always happened like this and he was no good with the telephone anyway, even when speaking to Pete. Should he try again? But there were now three people wanting to use the phone.

He put the card away, picked up his backpack and slid out of the phone box. Perhaps he would have more success at Numbers 5–9 Glate Street. He zipped up his coat. It was a cold day today and looked like rain.

The offices looked rather different from Saturday. Cars were parked all down the side of the drive and were packed into the car-park at the back of the three offices like the proverbial tin of sardines.

Stimps dodged around the cars bending low. He didn't want anyone to see him. They might suspect something. Boys weren't usually found on office car-parks during school-time unless they were up to no-good. He went straight for the space reserved for MT Trott. There *was* a car parked there today. A medium-sized, red, Japanese-made one. Stimps peered into the back; a pile of papers on one side and a child's booster seat on the other. Stimps frowned. He didn't expect MT Trott to drive a car with a booster seat. What next? Stimps thought.

He left the car-park and went back to the garages on the driveway. He could still see the back door. It would be useful to know if it was open in the daytime.

I'll just hang around a bit, he thought. After all, I've got all day.

By now it had begun to rain. Stimps needed some-where to shelter. The door of a garage was slightly open, so he slipped inside where he could have a clear view of the door.

He didn't have long to wait. A black car crunched down the driveway and parked directly in front of MT Trott's car. How does anyone ever get out of this car-park? Stimps thought. Out jumped two men, smartly dressed and holding big black attaché cases. They headed straight for the back door, up two steps and went inside.

So, it is open, Stimps thought.

He glanced at his watch. It was only half past nine. He'd got all day to pass. What was he going to do? He'd found out all he wanted to know. The rain was coming down steadily and even in the garage Stimps felt cold. He couldn't stay there all day. He stood for a couple of minutes uncertain of what to do. Perhaps he should go back to school. Find some excuse for being late.

Stimps genuinely did like school so this seemed the best thing to do. He hurried to the bus station, where to his relief a bus was about to leave. He was in his classroom just before ten o'clock.

'We were late getting up,' he muttered to Mrs Whiteman and turned away because he knew he was no good at telling lies and she was an expert at knowing when a child was lying.

But it was Monday morning and Mrs Whiteman was busy setting up the week's activities for the children. She simply said, 'Go and tell the office you've arrived, Robert.'

Stimps told Pete all about his discoveries over playtime. 'I didn't discover much but MT Trott drives a medium-sized Japanese car with a child's booster seat and the office back door is open during the day. I saw two men go in. And the car-park is really full up.' He paused and shook his head. 'But I made a mess of my call to Mr Granville. Anyway, I don't think anyone I know saw me.'

But that was where Stimps was wrong.

Just after playtime the school secretary was in the classroom talking with Mrs Whiteman.

'Mr Brooke would like to see Robert Stimpson,' she said as she was leaving.

Stimps walked into the headteacher's office wondering what exactly he could want. He didn't often summon children into his office. One look at Mr Brooke's stern face and Stimps knew he was in trouble. Mr Brooke kept him waiting while he finished writing something.

He took off his glasses and stared at Stimps.

'Robert,' he said coldly, 'can you explain to me why

I saw you getting on a bus in the bus station this morning at half past nine? But when you came in late to school you said it was because your family was late in getting up?'

Stimps groaned inside. He stared at his feet and shuffled them. What were the chances of Mr Brooke walking round the bus station on a Monday morning?! It must be one chance in a million!

'I can't explain,' he mumbled, still looking down.

'That's no answer,' Mr Brooke said.

Stimps hung his head.

'Well?'

Still Stimps said nothing. What could he say?

'Look at me, Robert. This is the second time I've had to tell you off in a fortnight. I don't know what's happened to you. First you are very rude to Mrs Whiteman and then you deliberately miss school. This is very serious, so serious I shall contact your parents to tell them about it. You can explain it to them. You'll miss playtimes for the next three days and stand outside my office.'

He looked up at Mr Brooke, miserably. 'I'm sorry, Sir,' he managed to say. 'It won't happen again.'

'I should hope not,' Mr Brooke said sternly. 'Now go back to your class.'

During the next three playtimes Stimps had plenty of time to think about the unfairness in his life. He knew he'd done wrong but . . . All the time he kept coming back to how unfair it was that Dad had to leave the shop.

On the wall opposite Mr Brooke's office were pictures of children who were refugees. The school was collecting clothes and presents for them. These children wouldn't be looking forward to Christmas, because they were in a country which was in a war.

There wouldn't be many presents for them. Many were starving and many were orphans. The more he looked at the picture, the more unfair it seemed to him that children in his school had so much, while these children had so little. What had *they* done to deserve it? Dad having to leave the shop wasn't the only unfair thing in the world.

Mr Brooke did speak to his mother on the phone. So when Stimps had arrived home that Monday, he had had a lot of explaining to do. But his parents weren't impressed at all. In fact, Dad had been very very angry; so angry that his glasses got all steamed up. He'd insisted that Stimps give up any plans to save the shop. Stimps was sent to bed early.

'And you'll go to bed early for the rest of the week!' his father had shouted after Stimps as he dashed upstairs.

After he had calmed down, Dad wrote to Mr Brooke to explain.

'I've done everything I can, Robert,' Mr Stimpson said to Stimps over breakfast the next morning, 'and there is nothing more we can do. Nothing. Mr Granville has made that quite clear. We may set up another barber's business. But if not, I shall try to do something else. Mum's looking for a job too.'

He gave his son a big hug as he left to go to school and told him not to worry. But he didn't look at Stimps when he said that, which meant he wasn't as confident as he sounded. He didn't smile either.

Stimps was not reassured. He couldn't stop worrying. He was sure he could do something if he only knew what. He still hadn't completely given up the idea of seeing MT Trott, in person.

Mr Granville's annoying phone call

Charles Granville hated Monday mornings. Everyone in the office was usually in a bad mood and often something had happened with the properties over the weekend which meant lots of work to be done.

He hung his coat up on the hook behind his door and sat down at his desk. His secretary had already piled up several files on the desk.

He yawned. I'd better make a start, he thought.

For five minutes he flicked through the papers, frowning every now and again. This made his scowling face even fiercer. He really did look like a bull-dog. He scratched his spaghetti-like moustache.

The phone rang. He picked up the receiver.

'Hello,' he barked.

'Call for you,' came the receptionist's voice.

'Charles Granville speaking,' he said briskly.

'Ah, ah Mr Granville, I . . . er . . .' It was a funny voice, like a child's, only a bit deeper.

'Who's that speaking?' he said impatiently.

'I . . . want to . . . it's about Grey's Yard . . .'

'Yes?' Mr Granville said. Do get on with it, he thought to himself, whoever you are!

'I . . . er . . . need . . .'

Irritated, Mr Granville slammed down the receiver. As soon as he had done that, he wished he hadn't.

But it was too late.

'Why did I do that?' he said under his breath. 'It could have been important. And I wonder who it was?'

But he knew what had made him cross. It was the mention of Grey's Yard. That barber's shop. It still made him feel very uneasy. He wondered what that call was about? And of course, he had no way of finding out who it had been. He hoped the caller would ring back. But no-one rang him all morning except his secretary.

It was a difficult Monday morning for Mr Charles Granville.

'You can't give up!'

'Coming over tomorrow?' Pete asked Stimps as they left school on Friday, three weeks later. 'United's match is on television and we could have a game of football afterwards, if it's not too dark.'

Stimps hadn't planned to do anything the next day so he readily agreed. He had stopped planning how to save the shop. It all seemed too impossible. There was nothing to be done. Unlike in his dream, the giant had flattened the ant.

The two boys settled themselves comfortably in front of the television, bag of crisps in one hand, can of Coke balanced on the arm of the armchair. The first half of the match was already over. It was an awful match. No goals and no exciting play.

'United's new manager has got no idea about what to do with the defence,' Stimps commented.

The door opened. In walked The Grandma.

'Hi Gran,' Pete called out without taking his eyes off the screen.

Stimps liked The Grandma in a way he rarely felt about an adult. The first time they had met, on that wet evening, she had seemed to understand him when he'd tried to explain why he was angry. After all *she* had knocked over a vase of flowers when she had been angry. She'd been treated unfairly. He smiled at her a little shyly.

'Hello, Robert,' she said. 'Enjoying the game?'

'It's awful,' he said.

'Mind if I join you?'

'No,' Pete called out, without looking across at her.

She lowered herself stiffly into the chair beside Stimps.

'I enjoyed watching football when my husband was alive,' she explained to Stimps. 'But it's only fun to watch it with someone else and once I was on my own, I never bothered. That's one of the good things about living here. I can enjoy football with someone else again.'

The three of them sat in companionable silence. Stimps glanced at The Grandma once or twice to see if she'd fallen asleep. Old people dozed off as soon as they sat down in front of the television. That's what his old grandpa (the Stimpson of STIMPSON and SON) had done when he had lived with them. In fact, he and his sister used to tease Dad that he was getting really old, because he often fell asleep in front of the television! But no, The Grandma was watching with interest.

'That's off-side,' she shouted out at one point.

Stimps was amazed. She really did know something about football.

The second half was as boring as the first. Stimps was glad when the final whistle blew. A goal-less draw!

Pete stood up and yawned. 'Nearly time for tea. What is for tea, Gran?' (His parents had gone out for the afternoon so The Grandma was in charge.)

'Go and see what takes your fancy,' she replied, easing herself out of her chair.

Pete dashed out of the room. The Grandma hobbled

after him.

'What's happened about your dad's shop, Robert?' she asked, turning to Stimps in the doorway.

'There's nothing we can do to save it,' he said. 'It'll close on December 15th. I've given up fighting.'

'Surely not,' she said shocked. 'Robert, you *can't* give up!'

Stimps shrugged his shoulders.

'Have you written to everyone you can think of?' she asked. 'And gone to see everyone you can?'

'Dad's written to the owner and all sorts of people like that and Mr Granville has made it quite clear that nothing can be done. I want to meet the owner myself but I don't know how.'

The Grandma frowned. She was obviously a great fighter, even though she was old and couldn't walk easily.

'I did pray like you said,' he added. 'I don't know if God heard because I didn't know what to say.'

'But you're not so angry, are you?' she asked.

'Well, no, I suppose not. But it's all so hopeless.' He sighed, 'I know there are loads of unfair things in the world and closing Dad's shop isn't the only rotten thing that's happening. But God hasn't actually *done* anything.'

'He doesn't always do what we expect,' The Grandma said, 'but he always hears us when we talk to him.'

'Let's have jacket potatoes,' Pete called from the kitchen. 'And we'll have a quick game of football before tea. Come on Stimps. It's not quite dark.'

'Put your coats on, boys,' The Grandma called after them as they raced for the back door.

The two boys had a good game in the garden and scored some impressive goals, even though by tea-time they were playing in the dark. It was much better than the televised match. They were starving when they came inside. The Grandma served up cheese, baked beans and coleslaw with the jacket potatoes.

Over tea The Grandma returned to the question of the shop. 'I've been thinking about you meeting the owner,' she said.

'You'll have to pretend to be someone else, to get inside the office,' Pete joined in, enthusiastically.

'Like what?' Stimps asked.

'Oh, the milkman or window-cleaner or someone like that,' Pete suggested.

'How can I be a window-cleaner?' Stimps said. 'Do ten-year-old boys like me clean windows in offices?'

'Well, no,' Pete had to admit.

'I'd have to go as a boy.'

'Like a paper-boy or . . . or . . . the son of someone who works there,' The Grandma said.

'That's it,' Stimps cried out, dropping his fork on his plate. It landed in the middle of the baked beans. 'I could go as Mr Granville's son. He's the only person I know who works there.'

'Does he have a son?' Pete asked.

'I don't know. Might have. He could even be old enough to be a grandfather.'

'If you went after school you wouldn't have to miss any more lessons,' Pete said.

Mr Brooke's face came into Stimps' mind. He did *not* want to miss any school.

'It's worth a try,' said The Grandma. 'And once you're inside the offices, you can find MT Trott and explain what's happened and perhaps everything can be changed.'

Stimps couldn't be so sure. If only Pete could come with him. This business had stopped being fun. He was the wrong sort of boy for this kind of thing. Boys who had adventures in books were tough and got things right. Robert Stimpson wasn't like that! He got his words mixed up.

He so disliked the idea that he put it out of his head. But time was running out. Christmas wasn't too far away. Plans for the carol concert at school were well under way. He'd even bought a Christmas present for his mum because he had seen some bargain perfume on sale in a shop in town. He hadn't got much money left after that to buy anyone else a present. He'd have to act soon or Dad's shop would be closed down.

One Wednesday evening, his mum presented him with the ideal opportunity.

'You're due at the dentist at 2 o'clock, tomorrow,' she announced as Stimps got ready for bed. 'Just for a check-up. I'll fetch you from school early and we can go into town together.'

Stimps found it hard to hide his delight. Normally he would have protested strongly at the thought of going to the dentist. But he saw that here was his chance to go to MT Trott's offices.

All night he planned how he could lose his mother once he'd seen the dentist. He had no idea what he would do once he got to the office in Glate Street. But you can only take one problem at a time.

MT Trott at last

'Perfect teeth, yet again,' the dentist beamed at Stimps. 'You should be proud of your son, Mrs Stimpson.'

Stimps squirmed. This dentist always treated him like a three-year-old. He never spoke to Stimps directly. Always talked to him through his mother.

'It's only half past two,' Stimps said outside the surgery. 'Is there any shopping you need to do in town, Mum?'

'I'd like to get some decorations for the Christmas cake', she answered, 'and then we'll go home, shall we?'

'Actually, Mum, can I do some shopping on my own?' Stimps asked, casually.

Mum didn't suspect anything. But these days she didn't seem to notice much at all. She was too worried about Dad and the shop.

Stimps said goodbye to his mother and watched her until she was out of sight. He then set off quickly in the opposite direction.

I wish I could go home, he thought. His stomach was all churned up, even worse than it had been an hour ago when he was waiting to see the dentist. But Pete (who was the only person who knew about his plan) would think he was a coward if he didn't go.

Pull yourself together, Stimps, he ordered himself. If

you're going to meet MT Trott, you'd better do it properly. 'And I hope you'll help me, God,' he added as an afterthought.

Snowflakes, just tiny ones, had begun to fall by the time he was walking down the drive at the side of Number 9, Glate Street. In the car-park behind the offices, he saw MT Trott's car, the red one with the booster seat at the back. He hadn't got the excuse that the boss was out. Already a thin film of snow was lying on top of the few cars that were parked there.

With a bold step (far bolder than he actually felt) Stimps walked up the steps and pushed open the back door. He stamped his feet on the doormat.

He was in a short corridor with a door either side and a flight of stairs at the end. He couldn't think why, but Stimps guessed that MT Trott would have an office on the next floor.

He walked briskly along the corridor and up the stairs, two at a time. So far, so good.

But luck was not on his side, for coming down, carrying an enormous pile of papers, was a lady. She was a very smart lady, in a grey suit wearing dangling gold earrings.

Stimps' first thought was to turn and run back downstairs. But that would look very odd.

'Could you help me?' she asked Stimps as though she saw him every day of her life. 'Could you open that door?' and she nodded towards a door at the bottom of the stairs.

Stimps tried to look normal. He jumped down the stairs and flung the door open for the lady to pass. At least she hadn't asked him any questions. He squeezed himself against the door, to make himself less noticeable.

But going through the doorway, the lady caught her

heel on a piece of sticking-up carpet. She tripped and the pile of papers spilt out of her arms and dropped, layer upon layer, on to the carpet. She swore under her breath.

At this point, Stimps wanted to close the door and run but instead he dropped to his knees and began picking up the papers.

'These are all mixed up now,' she said crossly. 'I shall have to sort them out again.'

Stimps hid his face as he picked up the papers.

'Who *are* you?' she asked suddenly. 'I don't think I've seen you around here before.'

Stimps took a deep breath and swallowed, nervously. He had hoped he wouldn't have to explain who he was pretending to be. Keeping his face down, he muttered, 'I'm Charles Granville's grandson.'

'Oh, I didn't know his grandson was so old. You've grown up quickly.' And she smiled at Stimps.

She believes me, Stimps said to himself, shocked.

'Your grandpa has the office next to the boss,' she said, nodding towards the stairs. 'I don't know if he's in today.'

So Stimps had been right. MT Trott's office was upstairs. As he handed her the last of the sheets of paper, he heard the sound of rushing feet and into the room burst a little girl. She couldn't have been more than four years old. Her head was covered with a mass of ginger curls, tied up in a large red bow. She was all in red. In fact, she gave the impression of a bouncing red ball. She darted behind the lady and grabbed her by the legs.

'Stop it, Rosamund,' the lady said crossly, 'or I shall drop these papers again.'

'I'm hiding,' the girl squeaked.

After dropping all her papers, the lady was in no

mood to join in any game.

'Stop it,' she ordered and stepped to the side.

Rosamund did exactly the same. Somehow she managed to trip up the lady and it happened all over again. The papers spilled out of her arms and floated down in layers onto the floor.

'Now look what you've done,' the woman said angrily.

But Rosamund skipped across the room and out through a door on the far side of the office. She didn't even say sorry.

Stimps sighed and dropped to his knees again to pick up the papers. The woman was muttering all sorts of things about the boss, and naughty children who were badly brought up and . . .

'Not many parents bring up their children to be polite like you these days,' she said. 'I'll have to congratulate Charles when I next see him. Which of his daughters is your mother? Celia or Jane?'

Stimps nearly choked. This was getting ridiculous. He'd have to chance it.

'Jane,' he mumbled.

The woman wasn't listening. 'That girl is the new boss's daughter,' she said with disapproval. 'Spends far too much time round here. This office isn't a nursery. Hmmmmm!'

Stimps handed her the last sheet. It was time he left. He didn't want to answer more questions about his 'grandfather' or his 'mother'.

He pushed open the door and set off up the stairs towards the boss's office, breathing a sigh of relief. Phew! He had escaped.

At the top of the stairs there was a corridor with a choice of three doors. One was labelled *Secretary*, another was labelled *C Granville* and the last boasted

Director, MT Trott. At last!

Stimps' adventures with the papers and Rosamund had calmed him down. With a boldness he didn't know he had, he knocked briskly on the door marked *MT Trott*.

Silence!

He knocked again. He must be in the building if his daughter is here, Stimps reasoned.

'Come in!' a voice called from inside.

Stimps pushed open the door and cautiously poked his head around it.

The carpet was a bright blue with three black leather armchairs in the middle of the floor. There were plants everywhere, on top of the cupboard, coming out of a large pot near the door and even climbing up the window frame. Stimps took all this in, in a fraction of a second. But his gaze was drawn like a magnet to MT Trott, sitting in one of the armchairs. He gaped. The door clanged shut behind him.

'Well,' the boss said, 'who are you?'

Stimps stared.

'Don't stare at me, boy.'

Stimps swallowed hard. He had been waiting for this moment for a long time.

'Excuse me interrupting,' he said, 'but are you the director of MT Trott?'

'Of course I am,' was the reply. 'Who are you and what do you want?'

Stimps took a deep breath.

'You own my dad's barber's shop, STIMPSON and SON in Grey's Yard and he's been told by Mr Granville that he's got to get out by next week because you want to modernise the shop. But Dad's got a lot of customers and he's never going to find another shop like this one.' It all came out very quickly, even though he had practised in front of the mirror a dozen times. He paused for breath, then added as an afterthought, 'I've come to ask if you *have* to close the shop down.'

MT Trott looked at Stimps.

'You've come here to ask me that?'

'I didn't know what else to do,' Stimps stammered.

'Well, *I* don't make decisions about small shops like your father's,' MT Trott said quickly, in a businesslike manner. 'But I'll have a word with Mr Granville, my agent, and see if he can explain it to me. Simpson, did you say?'

'Stimpson,' Stimps corrected miserably.

'Is that OK?'

Stimps shrugged his shoulders. Of course, this wasn't OK. Mr Granville would do nothing.

'He'll write to your father in a day or two. Good-bye.'

MT Trott picked a file off the floor. This had been useless.

'Off you go.'

But Stimps still hesitated. Was this how it was going to end?

'Excuse me,' he said, 'but Mr Granville hates my dad. He wants him out, ever since the trouble over Mrs Jenkins' wool shop.'

'Well, really!' MT Trott said, laying the file back on the floor, standing up and taking a step towards Stimps.

She was a tall woman with long, black wavy hair. Like the secretary she had dangling earrings and like her daughter, she was dressed all in red. She seemed a cold woman, not like Stimps' mother. Stimps couldn't imagine cuddling up to her. But he wasn't going to stay to find out any more about her. No-one had ever told him that the boss of MT Trott was a woman!

He grabbed the door handle, flung it open and

dashed out of the room – just as there was a scream from somewhere downstairs, followed by the cry of a child.

Kidnapped

Stimps was already racing down the corridor, to escape from MT Trott, when he heard another scream. He jumped down the stairs, three at a time, landing at the bottom just as the door near the foot of the stairs burst open.

Two men, with stockings covering their faces, flung themselves through the door, one of them holding a bundle of sacking. There was something red sticking out of it.

Stimps crashed into the second of these men and the two of them bounced off each other, staggering backwards. The man regained his balance first. He grabbed hold of Stimps by his coat collar and rushed after the first man, dragging Stimps with him.

Stimps was completely winded and surprised. This man was twice as big and strong as he was so at first he didn't even struggle. But once in the car-park Stimps began to swing his arms round, trying to hit the man. But he kept missing. The still-falling snow made the ground very slippery. Stimps found it hard to stay upright. His neck was held in a tight grip. He couldn't see straight because his face was forced down on to his chin.

The first man had already stuffed the bundle into the back of a rusty, white van. Stimps found himself lifted off the ground like a sack of potatoes and thrown into the van, after the bundle. As he flew through the air he heard the first man hiss, 'What you got him for?'

It was too late to struggle. The doors slammed shut, the two men jumped into the front, the engine came to life and the van roared away. It made an extremely loud puttering noise. There must have been a hole in the exhaust.

Stimps lay, out of breath, on the floor of the van, surrounded by oily-smelling sacking. He rubbed the back of his neck. It did hurt!

Everything had happened so quickly. He lay quite bewildered and then began to shake all over, especially his teeth. Where were they taking him? And why had he been taken? Who were they? Stimps had seen enough police films on the television to be certain that these men were criminals. He already realised his own life might be in danger. He pulled his knees up to his chin and squeezed them tight. At least that gave him something to do! If only the shaking would stop.

He couldn't see the men because the back of the van was blocked off from the front. But he could hear them arguing above the rattle of the engine.

'What you bring him for, you fool?' he heard the driver shout.

'He got in the way,' was the reply. 'I just panicked.'

The voices got louder and louder. Stimps discovered that if he tucked himself into a corner, he could be fairly still and wouldn't be thrown about so much. His own shaking had stopped. It was the juddering of the van which shook him up now.

Squashed into his corner he noticed pinpoints of light coming through rust holes in the side of the van. Stimps shifted himself so that he could peer through the largest of these. It was around half past three by now. It would begin to get dark soon but he could clearly make out where they were – heading out of town towards the coast. They would soon pass that shop he and Dad had looked at the other day. The ground all around looked a greyish white. Surely the falling snow would slow the van down.

He rubbed his neck. Ouch, that man didn't half hurt him. His neck would be stiff for days (if he lived that long!). He bit his lip nervously and stretched his left leg out. His foot struck the bundle, stolen from the office.

I wonder what it is? Stimps asked himself. What *did* these two men want to steal from the offices of MT Trott?

He shuffled nearer to the bundle and then to his amazement, the bundle jerked. And then it began to wriggle. It not only moved, it made a noise, a sobbing sort of sound.

Stimps threw himself back into his corner. What on earth was it? It was like a nightmare only worse. Because he knew for certain that this was not a dream. This was real life and here he was, Robert Stimpson, trapped in a van, hurtling through the snowy country-side with a monster for company!

And then, the monster sat up! It rose up out of the smelly sacks and moaned again, a long, low whine, 'Muuuuuummmmmmmy!'

Stimps did what most people would do, caught like this. He screamed. The scream was lost in the shaking rattle of the van. But the scream had an unexpected effect on the monster. It turned towards Stimps who became aware of two eyes fixed upon him. He swallowed twice, licked his lips and stared back. He stared and stared. The monster gazed back and then raised a paw and rubbed its head.

'My head hurts,' it sobbed. 'I want Mummy.'

Stimps immediately realised what this monster was. It was that rude little girl in the office. The boss's daughter! What had the secretary called her? Rosalind? Rosamund? Stimps could just make out her shape in the dark. She really did have a mass of red curls which stuck out all round her head like a pin-cushion. Her red bow had slipped to just above her ear.

Stimps was so relieved to discover that this was a harmless monster that he laughed. He leant over and patted her upon the leg which stuck out from under the sacking.

'My name's Robert,' he said as gently as he could above the racket of the van engine. 'I've been taken too. I don't know why, but we'll be OK.'

He didn't know they would be OK but it seemed the right thing to say. The little girl sniffed and wiped her nose with the sleeve of her dress. She sniffed again.

'Where are we going?'

Stimps sighed. He wished he knew.

'We're heading for the coast,' was all he said.

The girl sniffed, then mumbled, 'I want my mummy.' And to Stimps' surprise, she crawled towards him in his corner and cuddled up against his side.

Stimps also wanted his mum but couldn't say so to this little girl. He put his arm round her and there they sat, jolted along. She really was a very little girl. Gone was all the noise and bounce from the first time Stimps had seen her. The voices in the front were quiet.

'Is your name Rosalind Trott?' he asked.

She sniffed. '*Rosamund* Elliott,' she mumbled.

Puzzled, Stimps asked, 'Is your mum called MT Trott then?'

She didn't answer straight away. At last she muttered, 'Grandpa was MT Trott, but he's dead. Mummy works there now. Her name's Virginia Elliott.'

Ah, Stimps thought, that explained why the car parked in MT Trott's car-parking space had a booster seat in the back. But why would these men snatch Rosamund from the office? Had they kidnapped her?

'Do you know why these men have taken you?' he asked her.

Rosamund shook her head. 'Mummy will know.'

She began to cry again. Stimps squeezed her shoulders.

'Don't cry,' he ordered in a voice which sounded just like Mrs Whiteman. 'We'll get out of here somehow.'

But he felt horribly scared. Despite this brave statement, he had no idea *how* they could escape. The van rattled on. Surely, someone in the office would tell the police. Surely the police would chase this noisy old van and overtake it. It wasn't going as fast as a police car, certainly not in these conditions. But he heard no police sirens. No-one was chasing them. Nobody in the world knew he was here, even if they knew Rosamund was. Stimps felt very alone. This sort of thing only happened to people in books and certainly not to boys like Robert Stimpson.

He looked around the van to see if there was anything there that might help them. But unlike stories in books, there was no hidden key which would unlock the van door to let them get out. There wasn't a secret hole in the floor of the van. There was nothing at all, just two children and the smelly sacking. The holes in this van were only rust holes in the sides. But still, they were holes . . . Stimps wondered . . .

'Have you got a pocket?' he asked Rosamund, feeling in his own as he spoke.

She moved away from Stimps to feel both of her sides. She shook her head miserably. 'No. I'm cold.'

'Put this round you,' he said, pulling the sacking

towards them. 'It doesn't smell nice but it's better than nothing.'

Inside his own pocket he found a bright green mini boglin, which he had swapped that morning with another boy at school and a stubby pencil. Thoughtfully, he turned the stub round in his hand, peering through the largest hole in the van.

They were now driving through countryside with no sign of people or houses. There was still plenty of light to see by. But suppose . . . These two men, he reckoned, weren't very good kidnappers or he wouldn't have been taken by mistake. The second man just panicked. In which case . . . But they might be armed, with a gun or something . . . Was it worth taking a risk?

Mr Granville's grandson

Charles Granville had had no end of disturbances all day. People ringing him up, his secretary asking him lots of questions, letters to write and all the time he was worrying about the Grey's Yard shop. He'd got some work to do on that project this evening. The builders were ready to move in as soon as Mr Stimpson moved out. That was the end of next week. He would be glad when it was all over.

He picked up the receiver to make yet another call, held it to his left ear and dialled the number he wanted. He heard the familiar ringing tone ... prrrr ... prrrr ... prrr. But through his right ear he heard other sounds. Feet racing down the stairs, followed by a child's scream. Prrrrrr ... prrrrrr ... and then another scream. Prrrr ... prrrrr. More running footsteps outside his room.

Mr Granville sighed and put down the receiver. He'd better go and see what was happening. He stood up, glancing through his window as he did so. His room looked out over the car-park. Goodness, it had begun to snow. He had been so busy he hadn't noticed. Snow lay on the roof of his own car in the corner.

But the greater surprise was that on the other side of the car-park a man was throwing a brown bundle like a small carpet roll, into a rusty, white van, parked in the driveway. Half-running towards him was another man, dragging a boy by the coat collar. The boy was throwing his arms around as though he was trying to hit the man. This boy looked vaguely familiar but Mr Granville couldn't think why. The second man threw the boy into the van. They raced round to the front, jumped in and tore off, down the driveway, making a dreadful noise. Needs a new exhaust pipe, Mr Granville thought automatically. Only a few cars were parked today so there was nothing to slow the van down.

Mr Granville hurried down the stairs and out to the car-park. By the time he got there all the people who worked in the MT Trott offices had gathered outside, stamping their feet in the slush to keep warm. Mrs Elliott's secretary had an arm around the boss, who was crying. Whatever had happened?

'They've got your grandson as well,' the secretary shouted to Mr Granville.

He stared at her. His grandson, who was only two years old, was far away from here. What *was* she talking about?

'The police will be round straight away,' another of the secretaries said, joining the group. 'Unfortunately no-one got the number of the van. But it was so old and the roads will be bad so they won't have got far.'

'Will someone tell me what my grandson has got to do with this?' Mr Granville demanded.

Will the escape plan work?

'Rosamund, listen carefully,' Stimps said, bending over the little girl. 'Do you think you need to go to the loo?'

Rosamund stared at him. 'Why?' she asked.

'Well, do you?' Stimps asked her.

'Yes,' she replied after a pause.

'Good,' Stimps said, 'because I'm going to bang on the front to tell the driver you want to go to the loo. You can't wait.'

She stared at him.

'I hope this will work,' Stimps explained. 'I hope that they'll stop to let you go. And when you get into the loo, I want you to bring back as much loo paper or paper towels as you can. Stuff them in your knickers, up your sleeve, anywhere you can hide them. OK?'

She nodded anxiously.

'I'll wait here. You'll be OK,' he added, trying to reassure her.

Stimps turned to the front of the van and with a mighty thump banged on the partition. Rosamund's big eyes were fixed on him.

'Help!' he shouted. 'Help!' He hoped they could hear above the noise of the engine.

The van swerved slightly.

'What d'yer want?' shouted a surly voice.

'The girl wants to go to the toilet,' Stimps shouted

as calmly as he could. 'She can't wait,' he added.

'B . . . ,' the driver muttered.

The van jolted on as before.

Stimps waited a minute and then banged again, several times.

'She can't wait,' he shouted. 'You'll have to stop.'

The same surly voice said, 'Tell her we'll stop, soon as we can.'

They waited. The van jogged on.

'Do you know any numbers?' Stimps suddenly asked Rosamund. He didn't know how much a four-year-old knew.

'Some,' Rosamund muttered.

She wasn't feeling brave at all.

'If you can, try to read the number of the van, on your way back here.' He squeezed her hand, 'You'll be all right.'

She clung to him. Stimps could feel her heart beating. Her hand was all sticky.

The van swerved suddenly and screeched to a halt. The quiet in the van almost hurt the ears.

'Good luck,' Stimps whispered.

One of the back doors was unlocked. It opened just a chink.

'Get out, quick. Just the girl. And don't you try to run away.'

Rosamund scrambled out of the van. The door was slammed shut. Stimps was on his own. He peered through the largest hole. It was beginning to get dark. Where were they? In a car-park, obviously, because he could see a line of cars. They looked strangely the same white blob shape, all covered in snow. It must be a car-park in a town because Stimps could see a Pay and Display board and some buildings in the distance.

But he couldn't see a loo. Where had Rosamund

gone? He chewed his thumb nail nervously. Had he made things worse for Rosamund? She was so little. Suppose this was where the two men had planned to take her anyway? Suppose they locked her up in a shed? Or took her off in another car? Or shot her? And he'd be stuck here for ever. A wave of loneliness came over him. And fear. He wanted his mum or dad.

It seemed like ages although it was only a minute before the door was pulled open and Rosamund was pushed back inside. The two men ran round to the front of the van, their doors slammed shut and the engine groaned back into life. They were off again on their slippery way.

Rosamund was out of breath and shivering. Stimps could see snowflakes sprinkled over her red curls.

'Look what I got,' she said and pulled out of her sleeves several green paper towels. She lifted her skirt to reveal a thick wad of loo paper, caught in her knicker elastic.

'Is it enough?' she asked anxiously.

Stimps grinned.

'That's great,' he said. 'Well done, Rosamund.'

'And the number is 757.'

'You have been brave,' Stimps said. 'Now start pushing pieces of loo paper through that large hole on your side. Just a bit at a time, but keep pushing it through. We're still in the town and someone should notice us.'

She wrapped the old sacking over her shoulders and did as she had been told. Stimps meanwhile was frantically writing a message on the towels with his pencil.

Rosamund in white van 757. Help!

He wrote this on three pieces of paper towel which

he then rolled into a thin pencil shape, thin enough to be squeezed through the largest hole in the side of the van.

The van had stopped. Stimps' heart jumped. Peering through the hole he could see they were at traffic lights. People were hurrying along, wanting to get home before too much snow fell. He stuffed one towel through the hole. It fell to the ground. Surely someone would notice. Stimps put his eye back to the hole. Had anyone noticed? People kept walking along the pavement. No-one stopped.

The van jerked into motion. Would they stop again? He waited. They were still in the town. Rosamund kept pushing pieces of loo paper through the hole on her side. The van slowed down. More traffic lights.

Stimps kept his eye fixed on the hole and what he saw made him grab another paper towel and push it through the hole as fast as he could. It got caught and ripped on the jagged edge. Stimps forced it through and looked again. A policeman was standing beside the traffic lights on the other side of the road. Surely he would notice something strange. The policeman began to walk towards the van, looking straight at Stimps, or so it seemed.

Without thinking, Stimps thumped on the side of the van and yelled his loudest yell. Rosamund joined in. Their two voices sounded very loud in the small space at the back of the van.

The driver must have heard them because immediately the van moved. Stimps heard a man yell, 'Hey! Stop!' But the driver didn't stop. The van gathered speed, swerving first to the left and then to the right. Stimps and Rosamund couldn't get back to the safety of their corner. Stimps fell flat on his face, buried in the smelly sacking. One moment Rosamund was lying across him, the next she was flung into the corner. Were the men going to get away after all? His heart thudded.

'I'm going to be sick,' Stimps muttered.

And then he heard the sound he'd been listening for throughout this mad journey. A police siren! Not just one but two, maybe more. And they were getting nearer. The van raced on, swerving madly from side to side. The driver braked suddenly. Stimps and Rosamund were catapulted to the front. Stimps' head hit the side with a dull thud. He lay, stunned. The van swung round to the right. Stimps could still hear the sirens but everything seemed blurred. And then the jolting stopped. The engine stopped. There was silence.

He must have lost consciousness, for he never heard the back door being opened. He never heard the policeman say, 'And what have we got in here?' Nor Rosamund's answer. He never heard her begin to sob nor did he realise he was taken to hospital in an ambulance with a blue flashing light and a siren.

But once in hospital he remembered giving his parents' phone number to the police. But it was all very misty. Rosamund was taken away from him and he felt bad about that. He wanted them to stay together.

He lay on his back, his head aching. As he gazed at the ceiling, he realised that someone was standing at either side of the bed. He looked first at one and then at the other. It was Mum and Dad. Tears filled his eyes and rolled down his cheeks. He was safe. It was going to be OK after all.

Mum put her hand on his arm.

'Hello, Robert,' she said. 'What an adventure you've had. You can tell us all about it. But not now. I can't imagine how you came to be around the offices of MT

Trott. I left you to do a bit of shopping.'

'We've come to take you home, as soon as the doctor says we can,' Dad added.

Stimps felt too weak to explain. His parents were obviously so relieved to see him. He gave them a watery grin.

Soon after that, Stimps was allowed to leave the hospital and was driven home in the old red estate car. It was a very different journey from the one in the van. He sat quietly in the front, beside Dad. He wanted to tell his parents how scared he'd been and how helpless he'd felt. He wanted to tell them about Rosamund, the boss's daughter. And he knew at some stage he would have to tell Dad how he had met MT Trott. But to be honest, all he really wanted was to go to sleep.

The truth about Mr Granville's grandson

The group of people in the car-park of MT Trott's drifted back into the offices. Nothing was to be gained by standing around outside in the snow. Mr Granville soon realised that the brown carpet thrown into the van by the two men had been that awful child Rosamund Elliott. They had kidnapped her and it was expected that they would demand an enormous amount of money in exchange for her safe return. Her mother, after all, had become a very wealthy woman after the death of her father, MT Trott. Everyone knew that.

'I don't know how your grandson came to be mixed up in all this,' Mrs Elliott's secretary said to him, as they stood in the downstairs office. 'I'm so sorry. Have you told your daughter yet?'

The police had arrived and were asking questions.

'What's my grandson got to do with it?' Charles Granville said, even more puzzled. 'He's only two years old and is at home with my daughter, as far as I know.'

'It's your big grandson,' the woman had continued. 'You know, the one who was in the office to see you today.'

'But I haven't got a big grandson. No boy came to see me today,' he said, quite mystified.

'He told me you were his grandfather,' the woman

replied. 'Who was he then? I've been telling everyone it was your grandson.'

Mrs Elliott was talking to the policeman. She overheard them and interrupted, 'Mr Simpson's son, the barber in Grey's Yard, came to see me today. He left just before Rosamund was kidnapped. I wonder if that's who the boy is.'

Mr Granville stared at his boss. What was Stimpson's boy doing here talking to Mrs Elliott? Why did he say he was his grandson? At least that would explain why Mr Granville thought he'd seen the boy before.

'The boy's name is *Stimpson*,' Mr Granville told the policeman, stiffly. 'I have his address in my office. You'll want to tell his parents.'

They all waited. Every time the telephone went, Mrs Elliott jumped up to see who it was. But no news.

Mr Granville didn't see much point in waiting in the office. There was nothing he could do to help. He packed up his briefcase and went home. He had plenty of work to do this evening, including the final plans for the Grey's Yard shop, although the appearance on the scene of the Stimpson boy made him feel extremely uneasy.

It was all in vain

'You mean, you actually stuffed the paper towel through the hole in the van? And then, when you saw the policeman coming, you both shouted your heads off?'

Pete stared at Stimps with a mixture of envy and amazement. He'd come round the next day on his way home from school to see how Stimps had got on at MT Trott's offices. He'd no idea what an adventure it had turned out to be, although he suspected something had happened since Stimps had been off school.

Stimps was sitting in an armchair looking pale with an enormous bump on his forehead. This was turning into a multi-coloured bruise. He was feeling pale too and wobbly on his legs. He couldn't forget the shaking of the van; nor how scared he had been. He had felt so alone and helpless even though Rosamund had been with him. He never wanted anything like that to happen again. Never!

The police had been to see him that morning, to ask some questions. They had arrested the two men, who had intended to demand a ransom for Rosamund's release. Quite what would have happened to Stimps, no-one could tell.

'They didn't know what they were doing,' the policeman said, 'or they would never have taken you along as well. You helped save yourself and Rosamund.'

Stimps felt very proud of himself.

'We'll let you know what happens,' the policeman said as he left. 'Mrs Elliott may be in touch with you soon and the local paper will probably want a photograph.'

He was wrong about Mrs Elliott because Stimps' father didn't hear from her. But he was right about the photographer.

Before lunch two men from the *Evening News* called, one with a notebook, the other with his camera.

'We tried to get a photo of you and Rosamund Elliott together but her mother wouldn't let us even see her,' the reporter said.

They took Stimps' photograph and asked a few questions about the chase. But they were more interested in finding out about Rosamund. Stimps couldn't help. He didn't know much about his red-headed companion.

As the men were leaving, Stimps, without really thinking what he was doing, called after them, 'Did you know, my dad's shop is closing down at the end of next week?'

'Moving somewhere nice?' the photographer said, holding the door handle. He turned to walk out.

Stimps shook his head. At last, here was his chance to give the story of the shop to the *Evening News*. Perhaps it wasn't too late to save it.

He thought carefully. But it *was* too late for the door clanged shut as Mum showed the men out of the front door. They weren't really interested. Stimps shook his head crossly (only gently because it hurt!) and thumped the cushion beside him. He'd forgotten about Dad's shop in the excitement of the last day. But now he remembered. He had saved Rosamund. That's what the policeman had said. Why couldn't Rosamund's mother save his dad?

They heard nothing from the Elliotts. It was the last week of STIMPSON and SON. Stimps' father went to work as usual and was very busy. All his customers wanted a haircut before he closed down.

Stimps was back to school on Monday still feeling tired. He wasn't sure how to tell his friends about what had happened. And he felt upset for his dad. He was greeted as a hero. Most people had seen his photo in the *Evening News*. It had been printed on the front page:

BARBER'S SON SAVES GIRL IN KIDNAP DRAMA!

Not all the details were right but it made a good story. Everyone wanted to hear exactly what had happened.

'Were the men armed?'

'Did they shoot anyone?'

'Why didn't you try to escape?'

It was the last week of term so Christmas decorations had to be put up. Stimps' class was the oldest in the school so they had to decorate the Christmas tree and set up the crib in the school hall.

Stimps as the hero, was given this job. Every year he had walked past the crib . . . the shepherds, the kings, the donkey, Mary, Joseph and the baby. But he'd never looked at them closely. The figures had been carefully moulded out of clay and beautifully painted by children in the school some years ago. The baby Jesus was tiny as he lay on the stick-like straw.

He popped the crib beside Mary and Joseph and stood back to admire his handiwork. Should it be nearer the front? No. He'd leave it as it was.

That evening he walked down the alley to the shop. Syd's Sandwich Bar was open, lights shining brightly but no customers and no tempting smells. The light was on in Mrs Jenkins' shop too, the naked light bulb throwing its pale and watery light over the piles of dusty wool. Some men were standing inside but Stimps didn't stop to look. He hurried on to Dad's shop.

'Did everyone want to know what happened?' Dad asked, pausing in his work.

'Of course,' Stimps answered, 'I was the class hero for the day.'

He sat down, next to the two men waiting their turn. From when he had been very young, this had always made Stimps feel grown-up.

'The agent came in this morning,' he heard his dad say to his client, 'just to check up I was ready to move out at the end of the week. He brought in two of the builders who are going to develop the shop. They've signed the contract. The whole place will be gutted by this time next week.'

'And is this your boy who was kidnapped with that girl?' the customer in the chair asked. 'I read about it in the *Evening News*.'

Stimps nodded.

'And it was the owner's daughter that he rescued?' Dad nodded this time.

'They can't throw you out after that!' the man said.

'That's what people have been saying all day but Mr Granville made it quite clear this morning that nothing has changed.'

Stimps felt the helpless feeling coming over him again. It was all so unfair. The giant was going to crush the ant after all.

The last customer paid Dad and left the shop.

'Time for home,' Dad said sadly. 'I'll only do this four more times.'

He locked the door after them. Brrr . . . It was cold out, even though the snow had melted.

'Glad I caught you before you left,' a voice called to them as they turned to walk up the alleyway. Out of the darkness hurried Syd of the Sandwich Bar. His coat collar was turned up. His hair stuck out at the top like a broom.

'You haven't heard then?' he asked.

'Heard what?' Dad replied.

'About Mrs Jenkins?' Syd said.

'No, what about her? I never see her from one week to the next.'

Stimps moved closer to his dad. What was it that Syd knew?

'They've been looking around her shop, all day. Several men in smart suits with tape measures and clipboards. I don't know where she's been, but it's mighty strange.' Syd looked very grim indeed. 'I have this horrid feeling that they've done to her what they did to you. And I can guess whose turn it will be next.'

Dad said nothing, just stared ahead.

'These people get you in the end,' Syd said. He looked desperately miserable. 'I shall fight them all the way,' he added in a tone of defiance.

Dad nodded sympathetically. He'd never trusted Mr Granville. But he knew that this time, fighting would achieve nothing. Absolutely nothing. And if his son's escapade with Rosamund made no difference, what would?

Father and son walked to the battered red estate car.

'The policeman did say we should hear from Mrs Elliott soon,' Stimps said to his dad. 'Why haven't we?'

'Don't ask me,' his dad replied sadly.

Two days later, it was the school carol concert. Parents and grandparents had been invited. Every class made a contribution. Stimps' class recited some Christmas poems. It went rather well. At least, Stimps' mother thought so. She clapped especially loudly after Stimps had said his piece.

At the end they sang two traditional carols. Mrs Whiteman had made the whole school practise these for weeks and weeks. Stimps hadn't thought about the words when they were practising but this afternoon he stopped singing at one verse.

> *He came down to earth from heaven,*
> *Who is God and Lord of all,*
> *And his shelter was a stable,*
> *And his cradle was a stall:*
> *With the poor and mean and lowly*
> *Lived on earth our Saviour holy.*

He remembered the crib he had set up on Monday and the baby Jesus lying on straw. This baby Jesus who had come from heaven had lain completely helpless, just as Stimps had lain on those sacks in the back of the van. He had felt so helpless in all his efforts to save Dad's shop.

Perhaps The Grandma had been right. God had understood when Stimps had talked to him about feeling helpless and angry. God knew what it was like too.

The Grandma came to talk to him after the concert. She was keen to hear all about Thursday.

'Pete's told me but I want to hear it from you,' she said. 'When I encouraged you to see MT Trott, I never expected it to turn into such an adventure.'

Stimps told her everything, even how scared he had been. He hadn't told his friends about that bit. And he told her what he had thought when they were singing the old carol. He didn't mind telling *her*.

'And have you heard from MT Trott?' she asked.

'No,' Stimps shook his head sadly.

This wasn't going to be a happy Christmas for the Stimpson family.

A sad day for Mr Granville

That same day, Charles Granville was early for work. The office had settled down after the drama of last Thursday. The end of the week was nearly here. STIMPSON and SON's would finally be closed.

There was a note on his desk. He picked it up. It was from Mrs Elliott, the boss.

Be in my office at 9.30. V.E.

Mr Granville frowned. Whatever could this be about? Mrs Elliott hadn't been in the office since Rosamund had been kidnapped. He imagined several reasons why she might want to see him. A better job? Praise for the way he had handled the Grey's Yard business? A new office? He stretched out his long legs under his desk, planning the future.

Virginia Elliott was sitting behind her desk, waiting for him . . . not in the armchair as she had been when Stimps called to see her.

'Sit down,' she ordered coolly.

Mr Granville felt uncomfortable. This was not the pleasant interview he had been planning. Quite the opposite. She came to the point straight away.

'I have been most unhappy recently with your work, Charles, especially the way you handled the Grey's

Yard business. So I plan to change your job. As from now, I don't want you to work on Grey's Yard. This week several things have happened to make me look closely into what has been going on.'

Several minutes later a very miserable Mr Granville left her office. He had never expected this! He hadn't exactly got the sack but it was very close to it. Mr Granville was going to have an unhappy Christmas as well.

Are we moving?

'There was a phone call for you just before you came in,' Mum said to Stimps and his father on Thursday evening. 'Mrs Elliott,' she added. 'She said she'd ring back later.'

'Just to wish me happy Christmas,' Dad said gloomily. 'Some Christmas!'

They ate tea in a silence which was broken only by the telephone. Slowly Dad got to his feet. He was so slow, Stimps thought the phone would stop ringing.

'John Stimpson speaking,' he said, '. . . Yes, Robert's recovered, thank you. Just a bit of a bump on the head. He was off school on Friday. Yes it was awful, wasn't it? . . . I'm glad Rosamund's OK . . . You say, she wants to see Robert? Yes, perhaps we can arrange something . . .'

Stimps pulled a face at his mother. He wasn't sure how much he wanted to see Rosamund, not after all this.

His father was still speaking. 'Yes, tomorrow . . . Over thirty years. It was my father's business before he died . . . I beg your pardon . . . But we never knew. Not that we ever saw her. She never had many customers . . . Three weeks ago, you say? Was she in hospital? . . .'

Stimps and his mother sat at the table without

moving. Who was in hospital? What had happened? It sounded like Mrs Jenkins. Stimps and his mother fixed their eyes on Dad who was shaking his head in a dazed sort of way.

'This is such a shock,' his father went on. 'I thought when Mr Granville came in on Monday that was the end of the matter. You want to meet me tomorrow? Tomorrow lunch-time? OK. We can talk about it then. I'll see you tomorrow. Goodbye Mrs Elliott.'

He put the phone down with a clatter.

'You are never going to believe this,' he said returning to the table.

'Tell us, quick,' Stimps' mother said.

He took a deep breath. 'That was Mrs Elliott. The first thing she told me was that Mrs Jenkins died three weeks ago. We hardly ever see her so we weren't to know what had happened. Her sister found her dead in her bed.'

'Poor Mrs Jenkins,' Stimps' mother said. She had not often spoken to Mrs Jenkins but had always felt sorry for the lonely lady. So few people ever seemed to buy their wool from her. 'But that wasn't all she said, was it?'

'Oh no. Mrs Elliott went on to say that they're going to gut my shop next week. That's definite. But,' and Dad looked very dazed, 'as Mrs Jenkins' shop is now closed, Mrs Elliott wanted to know if I would be interested in moving next door. They would need to modernise it anyway so could easily adapt it for use as a barber's shop. She wants to meet me tomorrow lunch-time to talk about it, with her architect. And you'll be pleased to know that Mr Granville won't be working on Grey's Yard again. She obviously doesn't like what he's been doing.'

The family sat around the table looking at each other in a stunned way. At last, to break the silence, Dad said, 'I forgot to say, she said she was very grateful to Robert for looking after Rosamund when they were kidnapped.'

'I don't believe this,' Stimps' mother said putting her head on her arms on the table. 'Fancy nobody knowing about Mrs Jenkins. And fancy Mrs Elliott offering you this. I just don't believe it.'

Stimps left his parents arguing about the details. Dad was being proud and didn't want to have anything more to do with MT Trott. He said he didn't think he could trust them, not after all this. There must be a trap somewhere.

But Mum said that surely Mrs Elliott could be trusted. And how else were they going to manage? He hadn't got another job.

Dad said his father wouldn't want him to move next door.

But Mum said that his father was dead and wouldn't want them to starve. They were being offered a brand new shop.

Dad said he needed time. He couldn't make up his mind overnight. And anyway, it took a long, long time to plan and design a new shop.

Mum said he'd just have to make up his mind fast. He'd got no choice.

Stimps needed space to think. He let himself out of the front door and got out his bike from the shed. It was dark and cold but he'd zipped up his coat and tied a scarf tightly round his neck. The snow of last week had melted days before.

His mind was in a whirl. After all these weeks fearing the shop would have to close . . . after all he'd done to save it himself . . . He had been angry and helpless but now, at the last minute, it looked as though the ant had escaped from the giant's foot.

He cycled into the centre of town and then back again.

'I wonder what Dad's decided,' he muttered, as he turned into his road. A Coke can lay just outside the house. He bent down to pick it up.

I can put that in the recycling bin, he thought.

He put his bike back in the shed and knocked on the back door. He couldn't hear any voices although the light was on. He banged again. It seemed ages before he heard someone coming. The door opened. Against the kitchen light he saw the silhouette of his father.

'Come in, son,' Dad said, holding the door open for Stimps.

Stimps looked up into his father's face as he passed him in the doorway.

'Well, Dad, are we moving?'

In answer his father put his arm round Stimps' shoulders and gave him a squeeze. For the first time in months, Stimps saw on his face a big smile which reached the eyes behind the glasses. His father's eyes were almost glittering.

'Yes, Robert. STIMPSON and SON are staying in Grey's Yard. We're moving next door!'